Police Brutality

A National Debate

Police Brutality

A National Debate

Jerry Bornstein

—Issues in Focus—

ENSLOW PUBLISHERS, INC.
Bloy St. and Ramsey Ave.   P.O. Box 38
Box 777   Aldershot
Hillside, N.J. 07205   Hants GU12 6BP
U.S.A.   U.K.

In memory of Mildred McConlogue

Library of Congress Cataloging-in-Publication Data

Bornstein, Jerry.
    Police brutality : a national debate / Jerry Bornstein
      p. cm. — (Issues in focus)
    Includes bibliographical references and index.
    ISBN 0-89490-430-2
    1. Police—United States—Complaints against—Juvenile literature.
  2. Civil rights—United States—Juvenile literature. 3. King, Rodney—Juvenile
literature. I. Title. II. Series: Issues in focus (Hillside, N.J.)
    HV7922.B67 1993
    363.2'32—dc20
                               92-42146
                                   CIP
                                   AC

Printed in the United States of America

10 9 8 7 6 5 4 3 2 1

Illustration credits:
AP/Wide World Photos, pp. 6, 9, 14, 17, 21, 27, 28, 30, 32, 36, 40, 48,
58, 63, 70, 77, 81, 83, 85, 91.

Cover Illustration:
AP/Wide World Photos

Contents

This picture of the beating of Rodney King at 1:00 A.M. on March 3, 1991, is reproduced from videotape shot by an amateur cameraman. King is the one on the ground. One officer is striking him with a steel baton, another is kicking him.

1

Facing Up to
Police Brutality

George Holliday, a plumbing store manager by
occupation, was standing on his apartment balcony in
Los Angeles on the night of March 3, 1991, testing out a
new home video camera. In the street below four Los
Angeles police officers were viciously beating and kicking
a black motorist, Rodney C. King, as eleven other
policemen stood by and watched in silence. Holliday's
new camera worked quite well. It captured this sordid
event on videotape and refocused national attention on
the serious problem of police brutality.

On the night in question, Rodney King was
apprehended by police in Los Angeles after a high-speed
auto chase. King was initially tracked by a California

7

Highway Patrol officer. When he failed to pull over, she radioed for assistance as she chased him in Los Angeles.

When his car was finally stopped by police, King's two companions immediately obeyed police instructions to get out of the car. King, however, hesitated. When he finally got out of the car, he appeared to lunge at the officers and they then attempted to subdue him. King was struck by two darts from a taser stun gun, each with an electric charge of 50,000 volts—usually enough to subdue any suspect. When King still failed to obey police instructions to lie flat on the ground, he was struck repeatedly with police batons. In less than two minutes, King was struck with fifty-six baton blows and kicked six times. Then he was handcuffed. King suffered eleven skull fractures, brain damage, broken bones and teeth, and kidney damage, as well as emotional and physical trauma.[1]

Police brutality first rose to prominence as a national issue in the 1960s, with complaints about police abuse directed against civil rights demonstrators, ghetto rioters, and anti-Vietnam War protesters. While attempts have been made to deal with the problem over the years, it's painfully clear that the problem persists and may be worse than ever.

Police brutality is an emotional issue, with strident voices raised on all sides. Minority spokespersons sometimes condemn police with a broad brush. Those who minimize the problem sometimes tinge their

Police clash with student demonstrators at Columbia University in 1968. Several police and students were injured.

arguments with racism. Many people believed and hoped that a case as apparently blatant as the Rodney King beating might be a turning point in getting people to come to grips with this difficult problem. The images on the King videotape were so searing that many police officers around the country and even in Los Angeles, were embarrassed. Instead of unthinking solidarity with their fellow police officers, many policemen were being quoted in the press as expressing shock and disapproval of the King beating. The King videotape, just about everyone agreed, showed that police officers had gone too far. The old debate about whether police brutality was a serious problem disappeared. Now the question on the national agenda was how to keep such abuse from happening again. Some experts were saying that the history of the police in America could now be categorized as Before Rodney King and After Rodney King.

This debate on police brutality does not occur in a vacuum. It has a past, a present, and a future. It is intertwined with the problems of law and order, minority relations, legal rights of the accused, due process, and the role of police in society. The police are a special institution in society. There are many social institutions that reflect the state's intervention in our daily lives—from schools, to hospitals, to transportation—but the police play a special role. They are the only authorized purveyors of force and violence in civil society, the ultimate state regulator in social life. They wield violence but within the framework of rules. It is impossible to imagine a modern society without police, and impossible to accept a situation in which the authority and functioning of the police is uncontrolled and excessive. The great majority of police in America are not brutal. They are dedicated to serving and protecting the public. But there is a minority that goes too far and betrays the public trust, and gives a bad reputation to all police. There are whole segments of our population who do not trust the police because of the brutality of some. That is why the problem of police brutality is so serious.

There are many questions to be asked and answered: What are the causes of police brutality? How extensive is the problem? What can be done about it? It is a problem that demands attention and deserves a solution. There are many proposed courses of action on the table, from selecting, training, and retraining police officers to setting up civilian review boards and experimenting with new community policing methods, transforming the very way police interact with the communities they serve. What the outcome for America will be is still an open question.

Young people are often in the thick of the controversy, and as they grow to adulthood and take on the full responsibilities of citizenship they will participate in finding solutions. It's particularly important to understand the complexities and nuances of this issue in order to be able to contribute to solving the problem. This book will explore the problem, its background, and the possible solutions. It will suggest places to look for more information. It will be up to you the reader, a future adult citizen, to participate in the national debate to reach a solution.

2

The Rodney King Case Explodes

Rodney King was not a perfect citizen. At age twenty-five, he already had a criminal record—conviction for armed robbery—and was out on parole when he was stopped by police. Because of his record, if it weren't for the videotape shot by George Holliday, it's quite likely that some people would not have believed Rodney King's version of what happened that night of March 3, 1991.

The videotape was broadcast on Cable News Network on March 5th, and then rebroadcast across the country. Reaction was the same everywhere. From ordinary people to the president of the United States, everyone was shocked at what looked like a clear case of police brutality. President George Bush said, "What I saw made me sick." Police officers interviewed three thousand miles away in New York City were

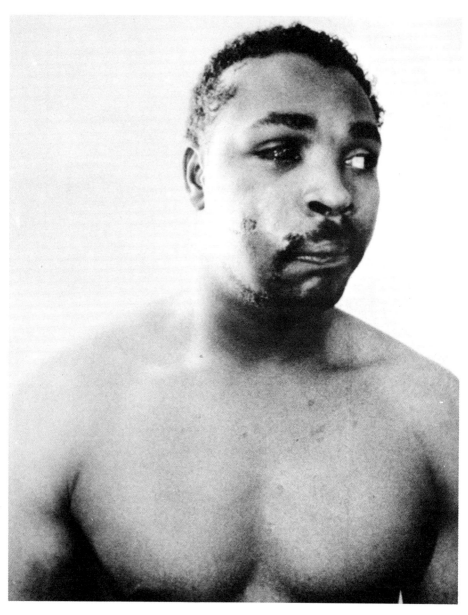

This photograph of Rodney King was taken three days after his March 3, 1991, videotaped beating by police. King's face is badly swollen from the beating. It was submitted as evidence in the trial of four Los Angeles police officers in Simi Valley, California, over the objection of defense attorneys.

embarrassed by the viciousness depicted on the tape. Members of the Black Congressional Caucus called on the federal government to take action. Then-Attorney-General Richard Thornburgh responded by ordering an in-depth review of more than 15,000 complaints of police abuse received by Justice Department officials over a six-year period. In Los Angeles, Mayor Tom Bradley, himself a former police lieutenant, appointed a special commission to investigate problems in the police department and make recommendations.

The commission, headed by Warren Christopher, a former Deputy Secretary of State, became known as the Christopher Commission. (Later, President Bill Clinton appointed Christopher as his secretary of state.) Its mandate was not limited solely to looking into the King beating, but included a general review of the problems of excessive force and racism in the Los Angeles Police Department (LAPD) as well. At the same time, critics called for the resignation of Los Angeles Police Chief Daryl Gates. Gates had had a long and controversial career at the LAPD. Many in the minority community accused him of condoning brutality and racism. Because of Los Angeles' unique city charter provisions, Gates was protected by his civil service status and could not be fired by the mayor. He could only be fired by the independent police commission "for cause"—gross incompetence or misdeeds. His critics said that Gates should take responsibility for the actions of his men and step down in order to restore confidence in the police. Gates refused, insisting that the beating was an aberration, not a typical event. Across the nation, police officers were embarrassed by the King case, and pressures grew for a reexamination of the problem of police brutality and how to eliminate it.

In July 1991, the Christopher Commission released its findings and recommendations. The report contained a damning critique of the LAPD under Gates' leadership. The Commission was alarmed by what they felt was "a tolerance within the LAPD of attitudes condoning violence against the public." They also uncovered evidence of prejudice against racial and ethnic minorities, women, and homosexuals. The Commission suggested that the current eight-hour cultural awareness class for new recruits be expanded. The existing system for reviewing and investigating police brutality complaints was also found to be inadequate. Commission members stopped short of calling for a civilian complaint review board, because they felt police would not cooperate with it. Instead they proposed a "civilian oversight process" to be set up under the umbrella of the Police Commission.

They also called for a revamping of the organizational structure of the department, making it easier to fire the police chief. Many of the proposed reforms were approved by voters in a June 1992 referendum in the city of Los Angeles.

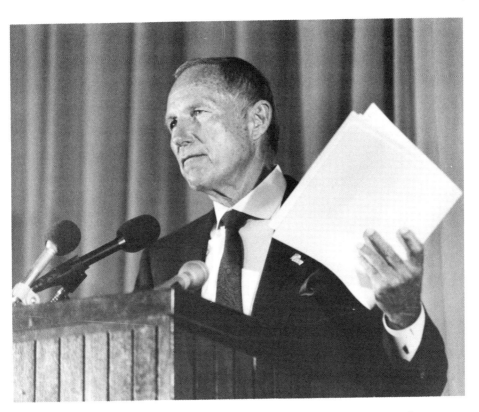

Controversial Los Angeles Police Chief Daryl Gates holds a copy of the Christopher Commission report on the Rodney King beating and problems in the Los Angeles Police Department. The report found a lax attitude toward police brutality and widespread racism in the LAPD, and called upon Gates to resign.

Meanwhile, four officers, Officer Laurence Powell, Sgt. Stacey Koon, Officer Theodore Briseno, and Probationary Officer Timothy Wind, were charged with criminal offenses, including assault with a deadly weapon, in the Rodney King beating. Their acquittal in April 1992 triggered the massive Los Angeles riot.

The trial was not held in Los Angeles. Defense attorneys successfully argued that a fair trial in Los Angeles was impossible because of extensive pretrial publicity. A change of venue was granted and the criminal proceedings were moved to Simi Valley in Ventura County, a predominantly white suburb of Los Angeles. Most legal observers believe the change of venue and the fact that there were no African Americans on the jury made the verdicts possible. While it's impossible to know what went on in the jury room or to read the minds of jurors, some experts feel that the jury was predisposed to be supportive of police officers and distrustful of black people like Rodney King. They point out that many people move to suburbs like Simi Valley to get away from poor blacks like King, and that many police officers live in the area.

In any case, jurors discounted the testimony of the California Highway Patrol officer who testified that she tried to stop the beating and took down the badge numbers of the officers involved in order to report them to authorities. They even discounted the testimony of one of the defendants, Officer Theodore Briseno, who said that his colleagues were "out of control." They did not interpret the videotape in the same way as nearly everyone else who had seen it. They were not swayed by experts who said the beating depicted on the tape was excessive.

Instead, they accepted the argument of defense attorneys who said that Rodney King was a difficult-to-subdue suspect who continually refused to follow police instructions to lie face down on the ground and led police to fear that he would inflict bodily harm. One juror later told journalists that King was "in control" of events. He kept moving, so they kept beating.

On April 29, 1992, the jury acquitted the four officers on most of the charges. They deadlocked on one charge, voting 8–4 to acquit Officer Laurence Powell of "assault under color of authority."

For a second time the nation was shocked by events in the Rodney King case. Public opinion polls showed that 86 percent of white Americans and virtually 100 percent of African Americans believed the officers were guilty.[2] President George Bush said "it was hard to understand how the verdict could possibly square with the video." He said that justice had not been done, and he ordered a Justice Department grand jury to consider bringing civil rights charges against the police officers. In New York City, Police Commissioner Lee P. Brown said that the videotaped beating was "unacceptable under any standards of law enforcement in a democracy."

As word of the verdict spread, rioting, looting, arson,

and murder erupted in Los Angeles. By the time it was over, 51 people were dead, more than 1,300 were wounded, and 12,000 were arrested; and 6,000 National Guard troops, 1,000 federal law officers, and 4,000 soldiers and marines had been dispatched to help restore order in America's second-largest city. Violence broke out also in Seattle, Las Vegas, Tampa, Atlanta, and other cities.

The rage that exploded on April 29 was rooted in decades of racial injustice, economic hardship, lack of opportunity, and conflict between minority communities and the police. A quarter century ago the National Advisory Commission on Civil Disorders (Kerner Commission) warned that America "is moving toward two societies, one black, one white—separate and unequal." The upheaval that erupted in 1992 showed that not much had changed since 1968.

Politicians, sociologists, and journalists will continue to debate the underlying causes of the social unrest and what to do about it for a long time—perhaps too long. But one thing is clear, whatever the complex social issues that threaten to tear our society apart: the flashpoint for the rioting was once again a case of alleged police brutality—just as it was in the riots of the 1960s. Too often, cases of alleged police brutality involve white policemen and minority victims. This only heightens the sense of racial victimization in the minority community.

On May 1, 1992, Rodney King appeals for an end to the rioting, arson, and looting that erupted in Los Angeles shortly after four police officers were acquitted on charges stemming from his vicious beating by police a year earlier.

Too often, the way complaints of police brutality are handled only seems to worsen this feeling.

In the case of Rodney King, authorities planned to retry Officer Laurence Powell on the assault charge, the one the jury had deadlocked on, but this plan was dropped after a federal grand jury indicted all four officers on charges of violating Rodney King's civil rights. Rodney King filed an $83 million civil suit against the city of Los Angeles and the police officers involved in the beating. King was seeking $56 million for medical expenses and for pain and suffering—$1 million for every time he was smashed by a police baton. He was also asking for an additional $25 million for future damages. And his wife was suing for $2 million.

The whole Rodney King episode has served to remind us once again how divided American society is on the question of race, and how much remains to be done. In the middle of the havoc as Los Angeles burned, the man at the center of it all, Rodney King, came out of seclusion and went before reporters for the first time since his beating in 1991. A large man, not used to speaking in public, he spoke softly and emotionally. "People, I just want to say, can we all get along?" he said. "Can we stop making it horrible for the older people and the kids? We've got enough smog here in Los Angeles to deal with, let alone setting these fires and things. It's just not . . . it's just not right and it's not going to change anything."

"We'll get our justice," he said.[3]

3

Police in America

As an institution, the American police department is barely 150 years old. The first organized law enforcement agency was the Texas Rangers, created in 1835 while Texas was still part of Mexico. On the municipal level, most major American cities originally relied upon night watchmen to preserve law and order, until 1844, when New York City organized the first police force. New York began with a force of 800 officers. They wore star-shaped badges made of copper, which quickly gave rise to the nickname "copper" or "cop." Other cities soon followed New York's lead: Chicago in 1851, Cincinnati and New Orleans in 1852, Philadelphia and Boston in 1854, and Newark and Baltimore in 1857.

In America, the police function is largely the responsibility of local government. The historical trend has been for these local political entities to establish new police forces as the country grew and the population spread to new areas. So, today, instead of having a centralized or coordinated police system in the United States, we have a proliferation of local police forces—more than 15,000 police agencies existing at the state, municipal, and county levels across the country. This means that the problems of police functioning, and especially problems dealing with excessive police force, can't be dealt with in a centralized manner. Solutions and practices vary from place to place, with innovations trickling down.

In *The Tarnished Badge*, historian Ralph Lee Smith has written that from the very beginning American law enforcement organizations were marred by corruption and public mistrust. In frontier towns in the American West, "the man with the fastest gun was made sheriff, to tame the other rowdies. Many western lawmen were themselves lawbreakers, criminals, killers, and fugitives." It was very easy for such "lawmen" to succumb to bribes and corruption. The image we see in old western movies where the local sheriff is bought and paid for by the local villain may not be very farfetched.

Urban police departments also had serious flaws. Several police stations were burned to the ground in New York City during antidraft riots in New York City in 1863. This indicated that it was not just compulsory military service in the Civil War that had rioters angry. There was also considerable antagonism toward the police.

Police brutality is not a new phenomenon in American society. It has been around since the first municipal police force was created in New York City in 1844. While today allegations of police brutality are often linked to racial incidents, the problem has not historically been simply a racial issue, but an economic issue. The violence that police have had to deal with since their very beginnings has been prevalent in the slums where poor people live. In the nineteenth century, this meant neighborhoods inhabited by Irish, Italian, and Jewish immigrants. In dealing with family violence and gang violence in these communities police sometimes resorted to tough tactics—long before the inner cities were predominantly black.

The close links between local police and politicians in the late nineteenth and early twentieth centuries meant that law enforcement agencies were often enmeshed in local political corruption. The big-city political machines and local party hacks often gave protection—for a price—to local criminals. Police personnel often shared in the spoils. To win promotions, police officers frequently had to bribe their superiors.

At the turn of the century, a police-political scandal in Minneapolis, Minnesota, showed how complete the corruption could become. Upon his election in 1901,

Mayor Alfred Elisha Ames fired honest police officers. Crooks from around the country were granted "concessions" to ply their trades in the city. Prostitution, gambling, pickpocketing, and other criminal activities thrived under police protection. The problem was not unique to Minneapolis, however. It was national in scope.

Over the next two decades pressure for police reform mounted, and during the 1930s, 1940s, and 1950s police departments began to reorganize. The first step was to depoliticize the police department, to separate police administration from city politics. Another goal was to improve the quality and professionalism of police officers. Until the 1930s most police were poorly educated; very few had a high-school education. Police investigatory methods were amateurish. Pay was low, which heightened the temptation of corruption. Efforts were now made to recruit better-educated officers, to boost pay, and adopt modern methods. Departments were restructured with a clearly defined chain of command, assigned responsibilities, and supervision.

Still, corruption continued. Dishonest police didn't need ties to crooked political bosses to figure out how to take bribes or make deals with organized crime. In Kansas City, Missouri, a grand jury in 1961 revealed the existence of an eight-year-old deal between organized crime members and the police department. The deal sanctioned gambling, prostitution, and fencing of stolen

These are two New York City policemen around 1920. In the early part of the twentieth century recurring corruption scandals prompted a growing movement for police reform. The goal was to depoliticize the police, recruit better-educated officers, and reorganize police departments on a more professional footing.

Police scuffle with striking workers at the New York Stock Exchange in 1948. The trade union movement and police have had a long history of clashing with each other, especially in the early days of organized labor.

merchandise in exchange for a guarantee that no major burglaries would occur within city limits. Another major corruption scandal, involving a handful of policemen who operated a burglary ring, occurred in Chicago. In New York City in 1972 the testimony of officer Frank Serpico before the Knapp Commission revealed widespread police corruption and a look-the-other-way attitude on the part of high-ranking police officials.

By the mid-1960s, however, police brutality became the main focus of public concern. While earlier in history, the labor movement often experienced violent confrontations with law enforcement, it was police mistreatment of nonviolent civil rights demonstrators, especially in the South, that had a big impact on public opinion. Televised scenes of police officers in Birmingham, Alabama, using high-pressure hoses and police dogs against civil rights demonstrators outraged the national conscience, and gave impetus to the passage of the Civil Rights Act of 1964. Similar atrocities were repeated in other southern cities. The same officers would seem to wink approvingly at the violent behavior of Ku Klux Klansmen and other racist extremists. In Philadelphia, Mississippi, the local sheriff and his deputy were accused of participating in the lynch mob murder of three civil rights workers in 1964. (They were acquitted on murder charges by an all-white jury, but were later convicted by a federal jury of violating the civil rights of the three victims.)

A Birmingham policeman uses a police dog against a nonviolent civil rights demonstrator in May 1963. Scenes like this, which were repeated over and over in southern cities, first focused attention on the problem of police brutality in the 1960s.

As the civil rights movement spread to northern cities, tensions between the black community and police escalated. In New York City in the summer of 1964, riots erupted in the Harlem and Bedford-Stuyvesant ghettoes after a black junior-high-school student was shot and killed by a white policeman. Over the next few summers, ghetto riots shook many northern cities, including Los Angeles, Detroit, and Newark. The incident triggering the riot was often a confrontation with police. It could have been a real or imagined case of police abuse—it didn't matter. An accumulation of social grievances made the inner cities a tinderbox, in which the slightest spark could touch off an explosion.

Political leaders found themselves caught in a raging debate between those who were terrified by the ghetto violence and wanted to give the police unconditional support for whatever methods they chose for quelling crime and disorder, and those who felt new measures were needed to safeguard against police brutality. In New York City, Mayor John Lindsay, a liberal Republican-turned-Democrat decided to create a Civilian Complaint Review Board to investigate charges of police brutality. This board, composed jointly of civilians and police officials, was designed to reassure minority citizens and others who no longer had confidence that the police department itself could fairly handle rising complaints of police abuse. The police union, rank and file police officers, and their supporters vehemently opposed the

In 1966 New York City Mayor John Lindsay appointed a Civilian Review Board to investigate charges of police misconduct. The men seated in the front row of this picture were the civilian members of the board. Those standing were representatives of the police. Mayor Lindsay is standing at the right.

board. They saw it as an attempt to tie the police force's hands in the war against crime. "Support Your Local Police" became the motto of a growing movement, composed primarily of middle- and working-class whites, that wanted to get rid of the Civilian Review Board. Eventually they succeeded in forcing a referendum in which New York voters rejected Mayor Lindsay's innovative solution. Later, a Civilian Complaint Review Board, which was more closely linked to the police department, took its place.

By the late 1960s the antiwar movement had brought hundreds of thousands of middle-class college students into the streets to demonstrate against the war in Vietnam. Clashes with police became routine events. Activists began to taunt police by calling them "pigs." Relations between police and a good part of the public they were supposed to serve had never been lower.

Following the ghetto riots of 1967, President Lyndon B. Johnson, in July 1967, appointed a special commission, headed by Governor Otto Kerner of Illinois, to investigate the causes of riots and to explore ways to keep them from ever happening again. The President's National Advisory Commission on Civil Disorders (known as the Kerner Commission) issued its report on February 29, 1968, and warned that America "is moving toward two societies, one black, one white—separate and unequal."[4] It said that the process of racial division could be reversed by a sustained and massive commitment of national resources. The Commission said that allegedly discriminatory police practices, unemployment, and inadequate housing were the most frequently cited grievances in the ghettoes.

About police-community relations, the Commission had this to say:

> The abrasive relationship between the police and the ghetto community has been a major—and explosive—source of grievance, tension and disorder. The blame must be shared by the total society.
>
> The police are faced with demands for increased protection and service in the ghetto. Yet the aggressive patrol practices thought necessary to meet these demands themselves create tension and hostility. The resulting grievances have been further aggravated by the lack of effective mechanisms for handling complaints against the police.

Written nearly twenty-five years ago, these words seem equally applicable today. The recommendations suggested by the Commission also closely parallel those we hear today: "eliminate abrasive practices" by police in the ghetto; set up improved mechanisms for handling complaints against the police; develop innovative programs "to ensure widespread community support for law enforcement"; formulate guidelines for police functioning in situations that could ignite community tensions; recruit and promote minority police officers.

All the unrest came to a head at the Democratic Party's convention in Chicago in August 1968. Antiwar demonstrators converged on the site to protest the Vietnam policies of the Democratic administration, led by President Lyndon B. Johnson. Police, backed up by National Guardsmen, forcibly cracked down on the protestors. Live television pictures beamed into living rooms all across America showed young demonstrators, most of them white, middle-class college students, chanting "The whole world is watching!" over and over, as Chicago police pummeled demonstrators with nightsticks. Liberal Democrats criticized the police on the convention floor, triggering an angry reaction from Chicago Mayor Richard Daley who defended his police. Subsequently a special panel assigned by the National Commission on the Causes and Prevention of Violence later reached the conclusion that Chicago officers had engaged in a "police riot." While there was obvious provocation by some demonstrators, the Commission found that officers were guilty of "unrestrained and indiscriminate police violence . . . often inflicted upon persons who had broken no law, disobeyed no order, made no threat."[5]

Now it was clearer than ever that police who worked the streets had to have a high degree of professionalism. They needed a level of expertise in dealing with difficult situations that had never been demanded of their predecessors. Police departments began to develop programs for sensitizing officers to social and cultural

Chicago police attack antiwar demonstrators at Grant Park during the Democratic National Convention in 1968. A special panel from the National Commission on the Causes and Prevention of Violence concluded that some officers engaged in a "police riot," attacking with "unrestrained and indiscriminate police violence . . ."

differences. They also began recruiting efforts to bring more minority members onto the forces. In 1968, President Lyndon B. Johnson signed the Crime Control and Safe Streets Act. Among other things this created the Law Enforcement Assistance Administration (LEAA), which issued grants to help upgrade and modernize local police forces. In the fourteen years it functioned, until being disbanded in 1982, the LEAA had distributed nearly $8 billion to local police forces.

Around this time, federal courts began to define more clearly the rights of suspects and the scope of police power. The most famous case was *Miranda* v. *Arizona* in 1966. The Supreme Court ruled that a suspect must be informed of his right to counsel during police interrogation and his right to remain silent, and must be warned that anything he might say could be used against him in a court of law. The suspect must also be informed that if he cannot afford a lawyer, one will be appointed for him. At first, law enforcement officials claimed that "Mirandizing" suspects would seriously hamper crime-fighting efforts, but there is no evidence that informing suspects of their rights under the constitution has jeopardized law enforcement. "Reading him his rights" is now a routine police practice. Some experts think that the Miranda decision has actually led to improved police functioning. Police have been forced to rely less on pressuring a suspect to confess during questioning. Instead they have had to develop better techniques in conducting searches and interrogations in order to gather evidence to charge suspects.

In 1973, in *Johnson* v. *Glick* (discussed in more detail in Chapter 4), the 2nd U.S. Circuit Court of Appeals developed a formula for judging appropriate and excessive use of police force. In 1985, *Tennessee* v. *Garner,* the Supreme Court ruled that a Tennessee law authorizing the use of deadly force to apprehend a nondangerous suspect who was fleeing the scene of a crime was unconstitutional. A Memphis police officer had shot and killed an unarmed fifteen-year-old suspect who had stolen ten dollars and a purse during a house burglary. The Court ruled that this constituted "unreasonable seizure" under the Fourth Amendment.

But despite the court rulings, the improved training and the higher educational levels of police officers, and the greater number of minority members on the nation's police forces, the problem of police brutality persists. African Americans and other minorities continue to complain of unfair treatment at the hands of law enforcement personnel.

Throughout the 1970s and 1980s there have been recurring charges of police brutality. There were even Congressional hearings on the subject. There was heated debate about whether brutality actually existed. After the watershed of the Rodney King case there was a new public awareness of the problem and renewed analysis of its causes and solutions.

4

What Is
Police Brutality?

By its very nature much police work is violent. Police officers are authorized by state law to exercise force to restrain and arrest criminals and to calm disturbances. Police brutality is the use of *excessive* force by police officers. Exactly what level of force is appropriate at a given moment in carrying out police responsibilities is often a subjective judgment. What's more, this judgment has to be made by police officers on a split-second basis under often difficult circumstances. What is excessive to one person's way of thinking may be necessary and acceptable to another. The same action might be considered justified under one set of circumstances, but under differing circumstances might be considered brutality.

New York City police wrestle a suspected drug dealer to the ground
in Times Square. Earlier the alleged dealer had broken away from
police when they tried to put handcuffs on him.

For example, suppose a criminal suspect was threatening to kill another person. And suppose that suspect refused to obey police orders to drop his weapon and surrender, continuing to threaten to kill. Under such circumstances—in order to save someone's life—if a police officer shot the suspect, it would not be considered a use of excessive force.

On the other hand, the same action—shooting someone—obviously would be excessive in a case in which a person merely didn't react quickly enough to an officer's request to move along. In the course of everyday police work, however, the contrasts between the different types of situations are seldom as clear-cut as the two just described.

In general, most state laws, court decisions, and police department regulations specify that the minimum amount of force required to get the job done—restraining or arresting someone—should be used. There are no simple formulas, since situations vary so much. Sometimes some gentle words of persuasion can calm a difficult situation and no physical force is required. Other times the use of a weapon is necessary.

Police department guidelines on the use of force are usually couched in vague, abstract terms. They often raise more questions than they answer. For example, the Los Angeles Police Department (LAPD) guidelines state:

> While the use of reasonable physical force may be necessary in situations which cannot be otherwise controlled, force may not be resorted to unless

other reasonable alternatives have been exhausted or would clearly be ineffective under the particular circumstances. Officers are permitted to use whatever force . . . is reasonable and necessary to protect others or themselves from bodily harm.

These guidelines raise some difficult questions of interpretation. What do "reasonable and necessary" mean? What is a "reasonable alternative?" How can you tell when "reasonable alternatives have been exhausted?" How can you tell what would be "ineffective?" How do you make all these determinations in a split second? It's not easy.

The court system has played an important role in setting limits for the acceptable use of force by law enforcement personnel. Criteria for judging excessive force have been developed in a number of federal court decisions over the last twenty years. One of the most important is *Johnson* v. *Glick,* which was handed down by the 2nd U.S. Circuit Court of Appeals and still serves as a model in most court cases involving charges of police brutality. In *Johnson,* the court said that police brutality is the use of an amount of force that "shocks the conscience," and listed four factors that need to be carefully weighed in each case in order to determine if excessive force has been used. The first is "the need for the application of force." The second is "the relationship between the need and the amount of force that was used." The third is "the extent of the injury inflicted" on the civilian. And the fourth is "whether the force was applied in a good-faith effort to maintain or restore discipline or maliciously and sadistically for the very purpose of causing harm."[6]

If we look for a moment at the Rodney King case, we can perhaps get an idea of what it means to apply these four factors. When King was first stopped by police he did not comply with police instructions to lie facedown on the ground. He appeared to lunge at the officers. Force was used to make him lie down on the ground. There doesn't seem to be much disagreement that there was a need for the use of some force in this case, as expressed in criteria number one. Except for some diehard critics of the police, most people tend to agree on this point.

The central debate relates to point number two: "the relationship between the need and the amount of force that was used." The prosecution in the King case argued that excessive force was used. After having been struck by two taser darts and four or five baton blows, King appeared to be lying prostrate on the ground. However, he was hit with a baton an additional forty-nine or fifty times and was kicked six times. Defense lawyers contended that when viewed in slow motion the tape showed that King continued to move, and because of his earlier erratic behavior the officers feared he would attack them. They claimed that the beating continued until he ceased moving, and that therefore the officers acted in compliance with Los Angeles Police Department policy and that excessive force was not used.

As far as the "extent of injury" is concerned, King's eleven skull fractures, brain damage, assorted broken bones and teeth, and kidney damage testifies to the severity of the beating he received.

As to the fourth factor, "whether the force was applied in a good-faith effort to maintain or restore discipline or maliciously and sadistically," prosecutors could point to the behavior of the officers after the beating. Witnesses testified that the officers joked about the King beating in computer messages to other officers, and that their written police reports misrepresented the severity of the beating. All of this can be interpreted as evidence that the beating was malicious and sadistic.

As the King jury verdict demonstrates, these principles for determining whether excessive force has been used are open to varied interpretations.

As far as the use of deadly force is concerned, especially the use of guns, police department regulations are often much more specific about what is allowed and what is prohibited. Again there is no national standard. What is permitted and prohibited may vary from state to state and even city to city within a state, but there are some generalizations that can be made. Police officers:

- are not allowed to fire warning shots or draw or aim their weapons at unarmed suspects who may have committed misdemeanors (a less serious category of law violation);

- are not permitted to shoot at or from moving vehicles;
- are prohibited from firing at an escaping felon who is not suspected of a violent crime, unless the suspect poses a lethal threat to others;
- may use deadly force as a last resort as self-defense against serious bodily harm or possible death;
- can use deadly force to prevent bodily harm or death of another person, to prevent the commission of a felony (a serious crime);
- may also use deadly force to apprehend a felon or subdue a suspect resisting arrest;
- may also use deadly force to suppress a riot.

To sum up, defining what is police brutality can be very difficult. The relevant guidelines and judicial criteria are all open to interpretation. Each individual incident must be examined, measured against the established framework, and judged independently. The decisions made by officers in the field must be made on a split-second basis. When the wrong decision is made, when brutality occurs, it is a serious breach of public trust.

5

How Extensive Is Police Brutality?

How widespread is the problem of police brutality? The answer has been the subject of a heated, emotional debate for decades. Some minority leaders and civil liberties activists charge that police brutality has reached epidemic proportions. Police officials and some academic experts dispute this; they insist that things have been improving.

The one positive thing about the Rodney King episode was that it showed conclusively that the problem of police brutality does exist. Even if there is disagreement about how widespread it is, it is clear that something needs to be done about it. As numerous studies indicate, the perception among African

Americans is that police abuse directed against minorities is a serious problem.

There is no national centralized office for handling police brutality complaints. Complaints are filed with individual police departments, local prosecutors, U.S. attorneys, the Federal Bureau of Investigation, and civil rights and civil liberties groups. There is no single clearinghouse to keep track. There is also considerable circumstantial evidence that many instances of abuse are not reported to any agency at any level.

Why? Sometimes people who are victimized are afraid to file complaints. Rightly or wrongly they fear retribution from police. Perhaps they are intimidated by complaint procedures that require them to go to the police department itself—sometimes to the very precinct house in which they were abused—and file complaints with colleagues of the officer they feel has mistreated them. Some victims of police abuse are criminals—drug dealers, child molesters, muggers—who are not inclined to file official complaints, and who are not considered credible witnesses.

It is also difficult to prove a charge of police brutality. Only a handful of the complaints filed are substantiated by investigators and result in charges being brought against the accused officers.

There is a whole controversy about why this is so. For one thing, the investigators are usually police officers, who may be disinclined to believe charges

Police in full riot gear stand by in the Crown Heights section of Brooklyn, N.Y., in August 1991. They were part of a 2,000-member police contingent sent in to restore order. Rioting broke out after a car driven by a Hasidic Jew fatally injured a seven-year-old African-American child.

against colleagues. In many cases the evidence boils down to the word of the complainant against the word of the police officer, and the officer is generally given the benefit of the doubt by investigators, especially when the complainant has a criminal record. Or, it may be that many of the charges brought by civilians are groundless. Whatever the explanation, the fact that so few complaints are substantiated may discourage citizens from filing charges. They feel that it is pointless to bother. For instance, in Chicago, the American Civil Liberties Union (ACLU) doesn't even bother to refer police brutality complaints to the city agency responsible for investigating them. "We just don't trust them," ACLU director Jay Miller told reporters. What this means is that the available statistics may seriously understate the severity of the problem.

The lack of confidence in police ability to investigate themselves may be well founded. In March 1992, the Gannett News Service released the results of a study on how police department internal affairs units handle complaints of police brutality.[7] They examined 100 brutality lawsuits, involving 185 officers, in which juries had concluded that police were guilty of misconduct and had awarded judgments of $100,000 or more to the victims. Police internal affairs units had cleared 111 in their own investigations; 29 had not even been investigated. In the city of Boston, a study commission discovered that in 79 percent of the abuse cases investigated, police did not contact any witnesses.

In cases in which the allegations are serious enough to require criminal charges being brought against police officers, the officers are often acquitted. Why? Jurors may be influenced to one degree or another by racism, or they believe police officers' testimony, or prosecutors may do only a half-hearted prosecution job because they don't want to jeopardize their close working relationship with the police.

While there are no hard statistics, there are a variety of indicators that can give us a glimpse of how serious the problem is. In the aftermath of the beating of Rodney King, Richard Thornburgh, who was then Attorney General in the Bush administration, announced that the Justice Department would undertake a systematic review of more than 15,000 complaints of police brutality received over the previous six years. The goal of the study was to identify any trends or patterns—racial, ethnic, or geographic. It's important to remember, though, that these 15,000 cases involved only complaints made to the FBI or to United States attorneys and did not include cases handled exclusively by local governments. The review dragged on for a long time. Results were leaked to the press in May 1992.

The report listed the police departments with the highest yearly average of complaints.[8] The Attorney General, William Barr, said that no discernible racial patterns to the incidence of police brutality were found in the study, although he said there might be a racial component. He suggested other studies be undertaken to address this question directly. According to the report, the department with the worst record was New Orleans, followed by the Los Angeles County sheriff's department. The LAPD (the city of Los Angeles Police Department) was eleventh. Cities with high levels of misconduct complaints seemed to be concentrated in the southwest, in a narrow band running from New Orleans through Texas to San Diego and Los Angeles in California. Leaders of police unions and some police commissioners dismissed the report since no effort was made to determine the validity of the complaints in the study.

At the federal level in 1991, there were fourteen prosecutions pending that involved alleged civil rights violations by police officers or departments. Twenty-two more cases were being considered by federal grand juries. Between 1988 and 1991, criminal charges were filed against ninety-eight police officers. Of these sixty actually went to trial, and forty-five were convicted. In 1990 2,500 complaints were filed in Chicago and 3,379 in New York City.

The controversy over statistics for New York City illustrates how complicated it is to figure out how widespread the problem of police brutality really is. Complaints in New York have declined sharply in recent

Cities With the Most Police Misconduct Complaints

(from highest number of complaints)

1. New Orleans Police Department

2. Los Angeles County Sheriff's Office

3. Jefferson Parish (La.) Sheriff's Office

4. San Antonio Police Department

5. El Paso Police Department

6. Houston Police Department

7. Chicago Police Department

8. St. Louis Police Department

9. San Diego Police Department

10. New York City Police Department

11. Los Angeles Police Department

12. Police of Puerto Rico

13. Dallas Police Department

14. Harris County Sheriff's Office

15. Oklahoma City Police

Source: U.S. Justice Department (ratings based on gross figures).

years—from a record high of 7,073 in 1985 down to 3,379 in 1990. Why is this so? Has the problem lessened dramatically? Or is the drastic drop due to something else? The answer depends on whom you ask. New York police officials claim the improvement is the result of special training programs instituted after complaints of police brutality during demonstrations in 1988 at Tompkins Square Park in Manhattan's Lower East Side. However, Norman Siegel, executive director of the New York Civil Liberties Union has told the press that the decline results from a widespread skepticism that the current Civilian Complaint Review Board will do anything about police misbehavior. "What these numbers reflect is the growing cynicism of New Yorkers," says Siegel. "More and more New Yorkers, mostly people of color and poor people, have lost confidence and faith in the board."[9] Siegel cited the low number of cases substantiated by review board investigators as a reason. In 1988, only 157 of 4,178 cases were substantiated; in 1989, 93 of 3,515.

Another indicator of the seriousness of the problem of excessive force is the amount of money that has to be paid out as a result of legal claims against city governments in brutality cases. For instance, Los Angeles last year paid $13 million from city coffers in compensation to citizens who sued because of police abuse. In New York in 1990, $9.3 million was paid to settle claims out of court for alleged police brutality. An additional $2 million was paid for false arrest claims. New York City officials insist that these sums don't necessarily mean that the police were guilty. The city figures it's cheaper to pay off than go to trial and risk an even higher judgment from a jury.

From another perspective, the argument can be made that the perception of widespread brutality doesn't match reality. According to this view, rising standards of professionalism and better training over the past two decades, have made police more judicious in their use of force. For example, Professor Sam Walker, of Nebraska University, has pointed out that "the number of people shot and killed by police officers has fallen by around 40 percent over the past two decades."[10] The number has dropped from about 300 per year down to 180. Walker believes this means that progress has been made in reshaping police behavior in terms of the use of deadly force. The next step is to focus more attention on reining in the use of nonlethal force. Otherwise the problem of lack of public confidence in the police will continue.

Some experts estimate that between 5 and 10 percent of America's 600,000 police officers may resort to excessive force in dealing with the public. That comes out to somewhere between 30,000 and 60,000 violence-prone law enforcement officers across the country. While this number is far too large for complacency, it does mean, on the positive side, that the overwhelming majority of American policemen and women are decent, law-abiding law enforcement officers who don't use brutality in the performance of their work. Charles Friel, dean of the College of Criminal Justice at Sam Houston State University in Texas, has pointed out that "hundreds, thousands of arrests are done competently." Friel doesn't believe that the highly publicized brutality cases give a true picture of what happens on the streets day in and day out.

6

Causes of
Police Brutality

What causes police officers to cross the legal threshold
and use excessive force? Many factors, some of them
closely interrelated, may be involved. Here is a brief
breakdown of some of the major factors involved.

The Stress Factor

Police personnel live very stressful lives. In addition to
the normal strains that typical Americans experience
every day about their relationships with their spouse,
their children, about financial problems, and so on, there
are also the stresses unique to the police profession.
Robert Scully, President of the National Association of
Police Organizations, has argued that part of the
problem of police brutality is the "stress factor" that is an

"inherent part" of police work. There is certainly considerable evidence for this argument. No one can deny the stressful conditions under which police officers function daily. American society has gotten more and more violent in recent years, and police officers put their lives in jeopardy every time they report to work. The homicide rate in the United States has nearly doubled over the past thirty years, up from 5 per 100,000 population in 1960 to 9 per 100,000 in 1989. The rise during the 1980s of ruthless drug gangs, often armed with automatic weapons more deadly than those carried by police, has added to the stress. Police find themselves fired on by suspects more and more each year since 1980. The number of police officers killed in the line of duty has declined only thanks to the growing use of bulletproof vests by officers.

The situation was summed up by former Los Angeles Police Chief Daryl Gates who said:

> We operate in a far more complicated and difficult arena than almost any other profession. Nobody else has to make the kinds of decisions that police officers do. Nobody else has to get his blood pressure and his pulse up so high, and then drop it down and make an immediate decision based on a variety of factors.[11]

Police Attitudes On Violence

One of the hazards of performing violent work is that violence becomes an integral part of the policeman's life

San Diego paramedics and fire fighters rush a fatally wounded police officer into an ambulance. Two policemen died after responding to a call about a neighborhood dispute over a rosebush. The assailant was also killed.

and psychological outlook. There is even a tendency for officers to sometimes forget that the power to exercise violence is essentially on loan to them from the state, and to think that they own that power. This can lead to a dangerous situation in which some begin to think that police officers themselves, as a social group, can decide when the use of force is justified, rather than society at large. In a study of the police force of a small industrial city in the early 1950s, sociologist William A. Westley found that officers morally justified the illegal use of violence that they felt was necessary.[12] Westley asked seventy-three police officers (half the officers in the city of 150,000 people), "When do you think a policeman is justified in roughing a man up?" Only 31 percent gave answers that were legally acceptable (when impossible to avoid, in order to make an arrest); 69 percent of the answers involved the illegal use of force. The most popular answer was: in order to gain respect. In additional interviews with police officers, blacks and poor white slum dwellers were identified as people most likely to need to be coerced into respecting police.

Similar studies conducted today get very different results. Police officers are much less likely today to openly justify the use of illegal force. What these results mean in practice is debatable. Compared to the 1950s, there is much greater sensitivity and sophistication today in regard to the issues of brutality, and even officers who might be prone to use excessive force may be less prone to openly admit their real attitudes. One study of police in southern California in the mid-1980s, for example, found that police officers gave much more conservative responses to questions about police use of force than ordinary citizens.[13] The answers given by citizens tended to be more tolerant of illegal violence by police, than did those of the police officers themselves. This led the sociologists who conducted the survey to conclude, "These policemen either have learned to report the correct attitudes or are significantly less favorable toward violence than a similar group of nonpolicemen."

However, the burgeoning uproar over police brutality and high-profile cases like the Rodney King affair, indicate that there still is a widespread problem about police attitudes toward the use of violence. In fact, a survey administered by the Christopher Commission, appointed by Los Angeles Mayor Tom Bradley to investigate the LAPD in the aftermath of the King beating, found that 5 percent of the officers believed it was proper for police to inflict physical punishment on a suspect arrested for a heinous crime and 11 percent said they had no opinion. With a total of 16 percent giving the "wrong" answer on such an illegal and inappropriate use of force, the Commission report said this was "evidence of a serious problem in attitude."

Policy and Practice Discrepancies

Another contributing factor may be the discrepancy

between official policy and actual practice in police departments around the country. Young recruits may be taught one thing at the police academy, but when they go out on the job they may quickly learn that things are not done according to policy. An "experienced" partner can undo many things learned at the academy. As Hubert Williams, president of the Police Foundation, puts it, "The problem is that sometimes training formally says one thing and the actual operation of the department says another. When that happens, reality often speaks louder than words." This problem of course is not limited to the police. The teaching profession, too, often finds a gulf developing between theory taught in teacher-training courses and what is done in the nation's classrooms.

Mixed Messages

Closely related to the official policy/actual practice discrepancy is the problem of mixed messages being given to rank-and-file police about whether brutality might be condoned by headquarters staff. While official policy always opposes brutality, the use of excessive force may be encouraged by a police hierarchy that seems to tolerate, or even reward, such behavior. For example in a Fayetteville, N.C., case, a federal jury found that the police chief had a policy of not punishing the use of excessive force. In Chicago, allegations are currently being investigated that "systematic torture" was used by a detective for nearly two decades in order to get incriminating evidence and confessions from murderers, rapists, and other violent criminals. Despite dozens of torture complaints against the officer, he was promoted and honored by the department. An internal police department report indicates police commanders were aware of the torture and looked the other way.

A contrast in response can be seen in comparing the attitude of Los Angeles Police Chief Daryl Gates to that of Chief Steven Bishop of Kansas City, Missouri. Despite official policy calling for the use of minimum force, Gates consistently gave his officers the "benefit of the doubt." In an August 1991 interview, Gates said, "If I think they were doing their very best to deal with a tough situation, and they used some force, and perhaps they got the last whack in" . . . and it can be "tough to distinguish whether the last whack was necessary. I give them the benefit of the doubt. I think they deserve it."[14] When the Rodney King beating occurred, Gates refused to accept responsibility for the incident, insisted it was an "aberration," and even refused at first to apologize to Mr. King. The implicit message given to rank-and-file officers may be that departmental leaders are giving the go-ahead to use more force than official policy allows.

By contrast, in 1990, Police Chief Bishop of Kansas City, Missouri, gave an example of decisive leadership in demonstrating that brutality by members of his force would not be tolerated. Within a period of a month, a

Former New York City Police Commissioner Benjamin Ward gave rank-and-file police officers a clear signal that he would not tolerate brutality. He not only disciplined officers who used stun guns to torture drug suspects, but also fired their commanding officers for letting such things happen.

Baptist minister and a priest had been beaten by police officers. Chief Bishop fired one officer and suspended the other without pay for six months. He then ordered a study of the problem of excessive force in the department, and then instituted a program to monitor and retrain "problem officers." There was no mixed message about what was acceptable in Kansas City. Police, from the cop on the beat to rank officers, understood that brutality would not be tolerated.

Another example of mixed messages can sometimes be seen in the way police performance is evaluated and rewarded. Promotions, raises, and recognition as "officer of the month" are usually awarded to officers for heroic actions. Often these have involved the use of force in making an arrest or breaking a case. Some researchers fear that the failure of police hierarchies to reward nonviolent performance of police duties encourages violent behavior and may contribute to instances of excessive force.

Racism

In a survey of LAPD officers after the King beating, officers were asked what they thought caused police to exceed guidelines on the use of force. Twenty percent cited racial prejudice as a contributing factor. If police officers themselves think that racism is a serious component of the problem, it cannot be ignored. Shortly after the King case broke, an article in *Time* magazine asked this agonizing question, "Is racism so pervasive among police that the fight against crime all too often becomes a war on blacks?"[15]

When it comes to racism, American society truly has a split personality. Most Americans subscribe to the classic American ideals of brotherhood, equality, justice, and freedom. These ideals have justified American participation in wars, and have served as the basis for legislation and social programs. Yet racism is perhaps the biggest blemish on the American national character.

Prejudice and discrimination have been directed against immigrant groups like the Irish, Italians, Poles, and Jews, as well as blacks and Hispanics. The existence of widespread ethnic and racial antagonisms in America, which totally contradict the national creed and America's self-image, is very much a reality in our society. Racial and ethnic stereotyping are everyday occurrences in the media, in the press, and on television.

If racism exists in our society on such a large scale, it is impossible to imagine that it does not impact on police. The fact that poorer, crime-ridden neighborhoods in the inner cities of the nation tend to be black and Hispanic, can reinforce racial stereotypes among police officers who are already tainted by racist attitudes. When someone who has racist attitudes, who tends to judge an entire group in a stereotypical way, also is mandated to carry a gun and a club, the danger of police brutality becomes very real. Racist attitudes dehumanize members of the target group, making them less than human. It is easier to heap abuse on someone, to be brutal to someone who is not really human. There is no way to know how many law enforcement officers in America are racist. The Christopher Commission found evidence of widespread racism in the LAPD, and many people in the minority community believe the police are racist. What is important is to take steps to neutralize the problem. In recruiting police personnel, psychological screening procedures must be used to weed out the racists. Cultural awareness programs can help chip away at the stereotypes that dehumanize members of other ethnic and racial groups.

Code of Silence

By the nature of their job, police often find themselves isolated socially and psychologically from the rest of society. A sense of internal group solidarity develops, a sort of us-against-them group psychology. In some ways this is a positive thing. Policemen perform dangerous work. A strong sense of solidarity with fellow officers helps people cope with this demanding profession. But one negative aspect of this group solidarity is the development of a "code of silence," or a "wall of blue" as it is sometimes called. According to this informal code, police officers will not inform on each other. This code of silence was initially revealed in the 1960s in New York, when it was shown that otherwise honest policemen considered it wrong to inform or file complaints against fellow officers who engaged in corrupt or criminal abuses. Officers who break the code and speak risk opening themselves up to ostracism and harassment from their colleagues.

After testifying against another policeman in an Ohio police brutality trial, one officer was demoted for allegedly leaking documents to the press (a charge the officer denied), and received threats on his life. Some experts feel that this code of silence contributes to an atmosphere that tolerates and even helps to spread the use of excessive force by some police officers.

American University Professor James Fyfe, himself a former police officer, has pointed out that the fact that the beating of Rodney King was administered:

> ...in public, and in front of so many other officers, betrays an absolute confidence that citizens' versions of what happened would not be believed and that other officers would not be informants. I don't think you can do that without working in an organizational culture that has let officers know that that kind of behavior will be tolerated.[16]

Problem Officers

Every police force seems inevitably to have a few "bad apples," officers with a psychological predisposition towards the use of excessive force. They manage to slip through the psychological screening tests. They may have bad tempers, a brutal nature, or racist attitudes.

Whatever it is, they are prone to get in trouble for using excessive force. Research studies have shown that there are a relatively small number of officers on each police force who are responsible for a disproportionate number of citizen complaints. For example, between 1986 and 1990, complaints of excessive force were filed against 1,800 Los Angeles police officers. Of these, 1,400 were named in only one or two complaints. But the Christopher Commission found that 183 of these officers were named in four complaints, and forty-four were the subject of six or more misconduct allegations. One officer, whose initial background report warned of a problem temper, was the subject of nineteen complaints, including three shootings, in his first two-and-a-half years on the force. In Washington, D.C., forty-four officers, or just one percent of the city's policemen, were involved in 25 percent of the complaints of excessive force.

Another aspect of the problem is the fact that most police forces around the country do not have psychological retesting programs, which might detect problems that develop over time—such as an inclination toward excessive violence. Weeding out problem officers is complicated by the code of silence that makes officers reluctant to inform on or testify against their colleagues.

Changes in Police Operating Procedures

Some observers believe that changes in the way police perform their duties over the past fifty years have created a situation that makes police brutality more likely to occur. Until World War II, most urban police patrolled the city by *walking* a beat. Patrolmen got to know people in the neighborhoods and the residents got to know them. In the post-war period, things began to change. The beat cop gave way to the patrol car. Instead of walking through the neighborhood, officers drove through, patrolling from their vehicles. This was a more impersonal method, but it was more efficient. Fewer police could patrol larger areas. More recently the transition was to the "911" emergency telephone system. Now the tendency is for police to respond to "911" calls, rushing from crime scene to crime scene.

These changes have led to a depersonalization of the relationship between the police and the community. When officers walked their beats, they got to know the shopkeepers, the kids on the street, the decent people as well as the troublemakers. When police knew the people in the neighborhoods, there was more likelihood of finding informal or nonviolent ways to resolve problems. Today, police tend to interact with the public only in emergency situations, dealing with crime victims and criminal suspects. Experts fear that this tends to make it more likely for police to resort to violence in performing their work. The more violence is used, the greater is the likelihood of slipping over into the use of excessive force.

Miami police head for their patrol cars. After World War II, the American beat cop gave way to patrol cars. This change depersonalized the relationship between police and the community.

Public Pressures

Closely related to the stress factor is the impact of public pressure on police to get the job done. Rampant crime and the drug epidemic in American cities alarms the public. Politicians from City Hall to the White House respond to this legitimate concern with political rhetoric, calling for "war on crime" or "war on drugs." Such slogans are catchy but can promote an atmosphere that encourages the use of excessive force by police. A "war" against crime implies a no-holds-barred struggle, where anything goes, so long as you defeat the enemy. Former New York City Police Commissioner Patrick Murphy has said, "There is no doubt that this war-on-drugs rhetoric is part of the problem—raiding all these crack houses, more guns on the street, cops getting automatics. It has cops so psyched up they think they are in combat." Nebraska University's Professor Sam Walker says that the war-on-crime rhetoric sends "a message to police officers that you can go out there and kick some butt, do whatever you need to do."[17]

In a democracy where even those guilty of the most heinous crimes have rights under the law, police being on a "war" footing does not relieve them from constitutional restraints.

Cultural Misunderstandings

Still another contributing factor is the question of cultural differences. In a complex society, a failure to understand and appreciate cultural differences among racial, ethnic, and religious groups can have disastrous results. This is true for ordinary citizens who have to learn how to get along with people of different groups with whom they work or live side by side. It is even more crucial for police, who have to deal with potentially violent situations. A police officer can misjudge a situation because of his or her lack of cultural awareness. He might overestimate, or underestimate, the level of danger involved in a particular instance—either of which could lead to big trouble. Likewise, knowledge of particular ethnic or racial groups can help police use nonviolent means to resolve problems.

In May 1991 in Washington, D.C., a riot broke out following a violent confrontation when two female officers attempted to arrest several male Hispanics for public drinking and disorderly conduct. One of the suspects reportedly lunged at the officers with a knife and was shot in the chest. Leaders in the Spanish-speaking community said that drinking in public is normal, accepted behavior in Latin America, and being arrested and handcuffed by female officers could be seen as an unnecessary humiliation to the suspects. While most Americans would agree that there should be no difference in the authority of male or female officers, taking account of the cultural implications of *machismo* among Hispanic males and attitudes towards public drinking could have avoided violence.

7

Solutions to the Problem?

Many possible solutions have been offered to reduce police brutality. Some of these are obvious answers to specific causes discussed above. Here is a brief rundown on some of the main proposals:

Police Leadership

The chief of police and the headquarters staff must make it clear that excessive force will not be tolerated. Officers must understand that they will be held accountable for their actions. There can be no mixed signals, no looking the other way. When violations occur, the guilty officers should be punished appropriately. When the signals are clear, rank and file officers can be expected to adjust their behavior accordingly. Many experts believe that this principle of accountability must apply to the police chief as well. While no one wants to go back to the old days when police departments were riddled with political corruption, it is important that the police department be clearly subordinate to civil authority.

Civilian Review Boards

Police brutality complaints should be reviewed by civilian review boards rather than by the police department itself. There is considerable public disbelief, particularly in the minority communities, that police department personnel will fairly investigate complaints against their colleagues. Many people think the police will cover up the wrongdoing. In many cities routine complaints are investigated internally by the police department. The most serious allegations are referred to the district attorney's office.

Of the nation's largest cities, twenty-six already use some kind of civilian review procedure, most of them established in the last few years. The term "civilian review boards" can be a bit misleading, however. The boards are generally composed of civilians and police officials working together. Investigative staffs are usually heavily drawn from the police department. Critics complain that these boards simply aren't independent enough to do the job right.

Some proposals suggest that independent, completely civilian boards with their own nonpolice investigators would better accomplish the job of restoring public confidence, and also give police the message that their behavior will be judged not by colleagues but by the public. There are also suggestions that a special prosecutor's office should be created to handle police abuse cases. The argument here is that district attorneys are caught in a conflict of interest in prosecuting brutality cases, since they have to rely on police cooperation to prosecute their normal caseload. This might make them disinclined to alienate police by vigorously pursuing cases against police officers.

Psychological Screening

Psychological screening procedures have to be strengthened. Too many "bad apples" are still slipping through and finding their way onto the police force. Officers with problem tempers and violent tendencies should be watched closely and rescreened. Persons with racist attitudes have to be weeded out, or their attitudes improved. Periodic psychological screening and counseling programs for officers already on the job should also be set up as well. The stress of years of police work, confronting violent situations, of having to put on a bulletproof vest every day just to stay alive, can be expected to take a toll on even the most well-adjusted officer. As Professor James Fyfe put it:

> A cop's job is much more dangerous psychologically than it is physically. But once a person becomes a police officer, they just throw

him out into this psychologically demanding environment and never look at him again.[18]

After its investigation of the Los Angeles Police Department the Christopher Commission proposed that all officers undergo rescreening for psychological and physical problems every three years.

Violence Reduction Training

All police personnel, and particularly problem officers, have to be trained in techniques of violence reduction. According to *U.S. News & World Report,* "some experts think physical presence and communications skills alone could resolve up to 98 percent of the incidents potentially requiring force." Nevertheless most police departments still emphasize training in the use of weapons rather than communications skills. Kansas City, Missouri, has been very successful with a new program to help officers with more than three abuse complaints in a six-month period learn communication skills. The course combines lectures, videotapes, and role-playing sessions. Officers learn that voice tone and pitch and body language are as important as the words they use in talking to the public. They learn about the importance of eye contact and giving feedback to people so they know that the officer is listening to them. They also learn that certain traditional parts of a police officer's uniform—such as mirrored sunglasses and leather gloves—may be perceived as threatening. The Kansas

Cincinnati police officer Michael Gardner in 1988 in his classroom at the Police Academy. Gardner instructed new recruits in the use of humor techniques to reduce tension in hostile situations. This is one of the ways to reduce violence.

City course has had good results, dramatically decreasing complaints against officers taking the course.

Miami was the scene of rioting in connection with alleged brutality cases five times during the 1980s. Since 1988 the entire 2,400-member Metro-Dade County police force has taken special courses in how to handle themselves in tense confrontations. Miami was one of the major American cities that successfully avoided rioting in the aftermath of the Rodney King verdict.

Cultural Awareness Programs

Cultural awareness programs help to overcome the problems that result from cultural misunderstandings. These programs are particularly helpful in improving police-community relations in minority and immigrant neighborhoods.

Legal Damage Suits

Currently victims of police brutality or their survivors can file for civil damages against the city government. These lawsuits can be very costly for city governments. Cities like New York and Los Angeles are currently paying out in excess of $10 million per year to pay off claims against the city for police misbehavior.

Some experts suggest that the rate of police abuse could be reduced by making individual officers responsible for the damages rather than the city. If an officer knew in advance that he would have to pay damages out of his own pocket, perhaps forfeiting part of his salary for years on end, it might go a long way toward discouraging brutality.

Modifying Police Reward Systems

Instead of giving recognition only to officers who perform daring acts of courage, usually involving violence, police departments should also praise behavior that reduces violence and still accomplishes the goals of police work. Some experts suggest that awards, promotions, and raises be granted in recognition of community service and innovative programs. Once a climate is established in which police feel they win praise and advance their careers by avoiding the use of unnecessary violence, it may help a great deal to discourage the use of excessive force.

Breaking the Code of Silence

If real progress is going to be made, the code of silence that keeps good cops from turning in the "bad apples" has to be broken. Blind loyalty has to give way to a sense of obligation to do what is right for the police profession as a whole. Protecting and hiding brutal police officers gives the whole profession a black eye. There are signs of progress. In Houston, most misconduct charges now come from police officers reporting improper behavior by colleagues.

Community Policing

Many experts believe that community policing is the wave of the future. This innovative method seeks to break down the barrier between police and the people in the neighborhoods they patrol. Citizens are encouraged to participate in the law enforcement process, working with police in a cooperative effort. A central ingredient is to bring back the "beat cop" of yesteryear, but at a higher level of expertise and responsibility. To overcome the depersonalization of police-community relations that accompanied the switchover to vehicular patrols, more and more police are assigned to walk beats in the neighborhoods. But under the community policing concept, the beat cops don't simply patrol the streets swinging a nightstick. They get involved in the community in a meaningful way. They may open storefront community centers, organize local anti-crime, anti-drug committees—even organize community demonstrations if necessary. Professor Fyfe has praised the community policing concept highly: "If the cop is part of the community and becomes a fixture there, it's good for him because he begins to see the neighborhood as more than just a bunch of people who call him when there's trouble. And it's good for the residents because the cop becomes a trusted institution."[19]

Community policing requires a major overhaul in the mindset of individual police officers. In contrast to

Children cluster around Officer Jack Cambria, who stopped by to chat in their schoolyard while on foot patrol. Bringing back the "beat cop" is one of the key elements in the highly touted community-policing strategy that seeks to improve ties between police and the people they serve.

the normal, military-like command structure that governs typical police work today, community policing emphasizes greater contact and communication between the officer and the people in the neighborhood. As Hubert Williams of the Police Foundation, has put it, "community-oriented policing requires the officer of the future to have greater discretion and to work with the citizens he is sworn to protect in a collaborative way."

Because it is such a drastic change from the way police work has been organized for the past fifty years, community policing has triggered controversy, especially among some veteran officers. Some officers complain that community policing turns them into social workers and hampers their ability to do real police work. The statistical evidence is still quite sketchy. On the surface, it looks like community policing has not reduced the crime rate. On the other hand, community policing has clearly improved police-community relations, and that has helped police to fight crime. Community residents are more willing to cooperate with and give information to officers they trust as a result of community policing efforts, and this helps police solve more crimes and make more arrests.

Another problem is that community policing is expensive. It usually requires hiring more police, retraining veteran officers, and making money available for the various community programs that officers will set up at their discretion. With many municipalities finding themselves in desperate financial straits during the

A Los Angeles police officer speaks to schoolchildren about the dangers of drugs. His visit is part of the effort to prevent crime and improve relations between police and the community.

economic recession of the early 1990s, money problems have become a major stumbling block in introducing community policing programs.

Recruitment of Minority Officers

Until the 1960s, police forces were almost all white. This contributed to the tensions between the police and people in minority neighborhoods. Not only did it make some residents feel that the police were an occupying army, it also made communication between police and the community very difficult. Following the inner city riots of the 1960s, the first real efforts to recruit African Americans and other minorities into police forces in large numbers began. Today police forces are much better integrated, but they are still not reflective of the communities they represent.

Minority groups now constitute the majority of the population in some of the nation's largest cities, but those demographics are not reflected in the makeup of the police departments. For instance, in New York City, the force is 25 percent minority, 75 percent white, whereas the city population is about 50 percent minority. Many white officers live in suburban areas outside the cities. Some people complain these officers are prone to carry anti-city-dweller, racist attitudes that are often found in suburban communities. New York City is considering legislation that would require officers to live within the city limits.

Recruiting minorities and raising the education level of police are both seen as possible solutions to the tension-filled relationship between police and minorities. New York Police Officer David Rivera, a Hispanic, also pursued studies at John Jay College of Criminal Justice.

Improve Educational Level of Police

Still another proposal to improve overall police performance and cut down on the problem of excessive force is to improve the educational level of police officers. Proposals currently before Congress would provide funds for advanced training of police officers and for financial aid to college students planning to make policing a career. One of the most controversial suggestions is to create a Police Corps, modeled after the Reserve Officer Training Corps (ROTC) used by the military for many years. Students signing up with the Police Corps would receive scholarships of up to $7,500 per year, a maximum of $30,000 for a four-year collegiate program. In return, the students would be required to work for a minimum of four years as a police officer. Proponents argue that this would bring more people with higher education into the police forces. While some of these people might leave the police after four years service, many could be expected to make policing their careers. And this would improve the quality of the police force. Those who leave would at least have gained a better understanding of police problems and needs. They would take these insights with them when they rejoined civilian life.

Police corps proponents argue that in the long run this would also benefit the nation's police. It would help police-community relations to have more people in the community who understood firsthand the problems the police face in doing their jobs. Critics complain that with so few dollars available, money would be better spent training and retraining persons who have made a long-range commitment to police work.

8

Five Major Cases: Were Police Guilty of Brutality?

The Rodney King case is perhaps the best-known police brutality case in American history. However, over the years there have been many other cases, in many communities. The cities of Los Angeles and New York often seem to get the lion's share of the highly publicized ones. But this does not mean that the phenomenon is isolated in these cities. If it were, it would be a much easier problem to deal with.

What follows is a quick rundown on five major cases that have received considerable attention in recent years. In all of these cases the civilians involved were black, the police were white. In each case, complaints of police brutality were investigated by local police departments and district attorneys. These investigations substantiated the charges of excessive force and concluded that the officers had committed unlawful acts. Criminal charges were brought by the authorities against the police involved in four of the cases; in one case there have already been two civil trials, and the police department is still considering disciplinary action at the time of this writing. In each case, the policemen were *not* found guilty in their trials. In two of the criminal cases, not-guilty verdicts were returned by all-white juries. One case was a non-jury trial, and the not-guilty verdict was rendered by a white judge. In the fourth criminal trial, the jury deadlocked at 11–1. The only black person on that jury was the sole holdout for a guilty verdict. And in the final case, the accused officers have been cleared twice in civil trials. This inability to prosecute criminal and civil charges successfully against white police officers heightens the sense of racial injustice that is deeply felt in the minority community.

ARTHUR MCDUFFIE

On December 17, 1979, Arthur McDuffie, a black insurance agent was riding a motorcycle in Miami on his way home from visiting a female friend. According to police officers on the scene, McDuffie ran a red light around one o'clock in the morning. Instead of pulling over, he led police on a high-speed chase, lost control of his motorcycle and crashed, sustaining severe head injuries. McDuffie died on December 21 without ever regaining consciousness.

After an investigation and an autopsy, four police officers were charged with manslaughter. The medical examiner found that the injuries suffered by McDuffie were not consistent with a vehicular accident, but rather were the result of a beating, with "long, heavy blunt objects." The four policemen were accused of beating McDuffie with batons and flashlights and then faking the accident to cover up what they had done. Each officer had numerous citizen complaints of abusive behavior.

Because of extensive press coverage of the controversy surrounding the case, a change of venue was granted and the trial was moved to Tampa, about 200 miles northwest of Miami. On May 17, 1980, an all-white jury took less than three hours of deliberation to acquit all four officers. Rioting erupted in Miami's Liberty City neighborhood, resulting in the deaths of eighteen people and $100 million in property damages.

ANDREW WILSON

Andrew Wilson was arrested at 5:15 A.M. on February 14, 1982, in Chicago on a warrant charging him with murdering two police officers five days earlier. The arrest followed one of the biggest manhunts in Chicago police history. The two officers had been gunned down shortly after attending the funeral of another officer who had been slain in the line of duty, and emotions were

90

Miami police detain three men (lying on the ground) who were caught looting during the rioting in the Liberty City section in 1980. Rioting broke out after four officers were acquitted in the death of black insurance agent Arthur McDuffie.

running high in the police department. The manhunt was so intense that leaders in Chicago's African-American community complained that police were rousting young black men at random and subjecting them to illegal interrogations.

A little more than thirteen hours after being taken into custody, Wilson finished a statement confessing to the murders and implicating his brother Jackie in the crime. After his confession, Wilson was taken to the central lockup at police headquarters to be held for a court appearance the next day. However, he appeared so seriously injured that officers at the lockup refused to accept him. At 10:45 P.M. Wilson was taken to a hospital emergency room, where he was treated for multiple lacerations to his scalp and face, bruises on his chest, and second-degree burns on his thigh. All of these injuries apparently had been inflicted while Wilson was in police custody. A physician at the county jail also examined Wilson and was alarmed by the injuries he observed; he reported the situation to the superintendent's office. It took headquarters three years to respond to that letter.

Later an internal Chicago police department investigation concluded that there was evidence that Police Commander Jon Burge and Detective John Yucaitis had tortured Wilson in order to get him to confess to the crime. Another officer, Detective Patrick O'Hara was accused of standing by and doing nothing to stop the torture. The officers allegedly beat Wilson, administered electric shocks to his ears and thigh, and chained him to a red-hot radiator.

In addition, the district attorney's office has information on at least seventy other cases of torture involving Burge or officers under his command, going back over the course of more than a decade. In fact, allegations of torture by Burge date back to as long ago as 1973, when a murderer named Anthony Holmes complained of being suffocated with a plastic garbage bag and subjected to electric shocks. Since the victims of brutality in these cases were criminals—murderers, drug dealers, and so on—they were disbelieved by authorities for many years. Burge and his colleagues denied totally the allegations against them. Twice civil actions were brought to trial involving the Andrew Wilson case. These trials pitted the word of a convicted murderer against three police officers, and ended with the officers being cleared. Because of public outcry, however, the police superintendent then suspended Burge and the other officers, pending proceedings to fire them from the force, a process that is still in progress.

ELEANOR BUMPURS

Eleanor Bumpurs, an emotionally disturbed sixty-six-year-old black grandmother, was killed by a policeman during an eviction in a Bronx, New York, housing project on October 29, 1984. After housing authority police and officials had been unsuccessful in trying to convince Mrs. Bumpers to vacate her apartment after nonpayment of rent for four months, a team from the Police Emergency Squad was called in. When Mrs. Bumpurs continued to ignore police instructions, officers broke in the door in order to physically enforce the eviction and remove the woman from the premises. As they entered the apartment Mrs. Bumpurs was brandishing a kitchen knife. Believing that she was threatening to attack one of his colleagues, one of the officers fired a shotgun at Mrs. Bumpers. The blast blew away two fingers on the hand holding the knife. The officer said that Mrs. Bumpers continued to grasp the knife in her injured hand and threatened to attack, so he fired again, hitting her in the chest. She died twenty minutes later.

Prosecutors said that the officer used excessive force. The first shotgun blast, they argued, had disarmed the woman and the second, and fatal, blast was totally unnecessary. The wounded woman could have been restrained by police; there was no need for her to die. Charges of criminally negligent homicide and second-degree manslaughter were filed against the policeman. The officer chose a nonjury trial, and the case was heard by a judge. The judge concluded that the prosecution had not proven the second shot was "legally unjustifiable" beyond a reasonable doubt.

Afterwards, the New York City Police Department modified its procedures for dealing with emotionally disturbed persons. The new procedures emphasized nonviolent persuasion and negotiation, rather than the use of force. It is also now required that higher ranking officers take over direct supervision in incidents involving disturbed persons.

PHILLIP PANNELL

On April 10, 1990, Phillip Pannell, a sixteen-year-old African American, was shot in the back by a policeman in Teaneck, New Jersey, a racially integrated suburb of New York City. Police originally arrived on the scene in response to a telephoned report that a teenager with a gun had been seen near a local high school. An officer accosted Pannell and patted down the teenager's jacket. He felt a gun in the jacket pocket and called out to his partner. Pannell then bolted and ran away, with the police in pursuit. The officers testified that Pannell twice turned toward them with his hand in the pocket where the gun was, as if to shoot. One of the officers fired at the fleeing teenager. The first shot missed. The second, fired a few seconds later, struck Pannell in the back, wounding him fatally. Police found a loaded, modified starter's pistol in Pannell's jacket. Witnesses at the scene insisted that Pannell's arms were raised and that he was surrendering when the officer fired the second shot.

The officer was charged with manslaughter. A medical examiner testifying for the prosecution said that the fatal wound occurred with Pannell's hands raised. A medical expert testifying for the defense disputed this, saying it was impossible to determine the position of the victim's hands. A controversy over possible tampering with the evidence erupted at the trial when it was disclosed that one of the bullets in Pannell's gun had a scrape mark on it. Defense attorneys said that this proved that Pannell had attempted to shoot the gun, that the firing pin had failed to function properly, and that the officer had correctly fired in self-defense. However, no damage had been observed on any of the bullets during the initial investigation of the incident. This led to complaints that police officers had tampered with the evidence in order to bolster their comrade's legal defense.

It took an all-white jury, which included two persons who had relatives who were police officers, eight hours of deliberation to acquit the officer in February 1992. Pannell's family has filed a civil suit for civil rights violations in the incident.

DON JACKSON

On January 14, 1989, Don Jackson, a black police sergeant on leave from the Hawthorne, California police force and a self-styled crusader against police brutality, conducted a "sting" operation in Long Beach, California. Jackson rode as a passenger in a car driven by a friend. Their car was followed by an NBC News television crew, with a hidden camera, in another vehicle. Jackson's car was stopped by police in Long Beach, California, for not holding its lane in traffic. In an incident that was captured on NBC videotape, Jackson got into an argument with one of the white police officers, who arrested Jackson and appeared to push his head through a plate glass window. The tape was shown the next morning on NBC's *Today Show* and triggered a community uproar. The Long Beach district attorney launched an investigation. Criminal charges against Jackson were dropped. The two arresting officers were charged with assault and with falsifying a police report. However, they applied for a disability pension because of stress related to the Jackson case. They were granted a pension that will pay them half-pay for the rest of their lives. Critics of the police department complained that this gave a mixed message to police, appearing to reward financially the accused officers.

Criminal proceedings against the officers ended with a jury deadlocked 11–1 in favor of acquittal. Using a tactic very similar to the one used by lawyers in the Rodney King case, defense lawyers ran the videotape in slow motion. They convinced jurors that the glass was broken by Jackson's elbows, not his head, and that the incident was a terrible accident. The juror who believed that the officers were guilty was the only black person on the panel. Rather than retry the case, charges were dropped.

9

Joining the Debate

America today is at a turning point. We can no longer ignore the problem of police brutality. Twenty-five years ago, the Kerner Commission made proposals about dealing with the poverty and despair that give rise to crime and violence, and also about how to improve the "abrasive" relations between minorities and the police. Sadly, the situation today is still too much like it was in 1968. Some would argue that it's even worse.

The problems of crime, violence, and tensions between police and the community belong to all of us. And we must all participate in the solution. No one needs the help of police more than the people who live in the inner cities. They are the biggest victims of violent crime. Yet it is here that the antagonism between police and community is greatest. It is a contradiction that can't be allowed to continue.

Many people hope that the Rodney King affair will serve as the catalyst for the dawn of a new era in police-community relations. The overwhelming majority of American police officers are sincere men and women dedicated to serving and protecting their fellow citizens. Their job takes a terrible toll on them physically and psychologically. Violence is part of their everyday lives, and yet they must exercise it themselves within proscribed, legal limits.

A minority of them are prone to brutal behavior. They are bad cops who give the whole profession a bad name. It is time that police and community work together to get rid of brutal cops. The misplaced sense of brotherhood that keeps good officers from turning in the rotten apples has to end. Community and police must work together.

It will not be easy. There is a public debate today over what to do about this problem that will undoubtedly go on for a long time. This book is meant to serve as a starting point for young people to begin to participate in this debate.

Police Chronology

1844— First U.S. police department organized in New York City.

1894— Police corruption scandal in New York City breaks, revealing that police promotions were received through bribes and political influence.

1902— Police corruption scandal in Minneapolis shocks the nation.

1925— Los Angeles City charter marks new milestone in police reform by separating police department from City Hall.

1950s—The "beat cop" gives way to patrol by police car.

1963— Brutality by southern police against civil rights demonstrators shocks the nation.

1964— First ghetto riots break out in New York City.

1965
-1967— Ghetto riots hit major American cities.

1966— A series of Supreme Court decisions strengthening the rights of the accused culminates in *Miranda* v. *Arizona*, which says suspects must be advised of their rights at time of arrest.

1968— President Lyndon B. Johnson signs legislation

creating the Law Enforcement Assistance Administration.

National Advisory Commission on Civil Disorders (Kerner Commission) proposes major reforms in police practices.

Chicago police stage "a police riot" in violent confrontation with antiwar protesters at Democratic Convention.

1970s—American police departments adopt the "911" emergency notification system.

Key court decisions help define the limits of legitimate police violence.

1972— Knapp Commission hearings in New York City reveal reports of widespread police corruption.

1980— Charges of police brutality, especially against minorities, grow.

Rioting erupts in Miami following acquittal of officers accused in death of black motorcyclist Arthur McDuffie.

1987— More than 100 charges of brutality are brought against New York City police following violence at a nighttime demonstration at Tompkins Square Park. Police officers are accused of beating an amateur video cameraman who videotaped the beatings.

Late 1980s More and more police departments implement violence-reduction training courses and community-policing experiments to improve police-community relations.

1991— Los Angeles Police beating of Rodney King is captured on videotape by amateur cameraman.

Federal government launches study of misconduct complaints against police.

1992— Four officers accused of assaulting Rodney King are acquitted by a jury that had no blacks on it. Rioting breaks out in Los Angeles and a dozen other major cities.

Notes

1. For a complete account of the Rodney King beating, see H. Tobar and R. L. Colvin, "Witnesses Depict Relentless Beating by Police," *Los Angeles Times*, March 7, 1991. Metro Section p. 1, and "The Rodney King Affair," *Los Angeles Times*, March 24, 1991, pt. B, p. 1.

2. *USA Today* poll reported in "Agreement on King," *USA Today*, May 1, 1992.

3. "King Chokes Back Tears, Calls for End to Violence," *Washington Post*, May 2, 1992, p. A1.

4. For the complete text of the Kerner Commission Report see Kerner Commission, *Report on the National Advisory Commission on Civil Disorders* (New York: Bantam Books, 1968). An excellent summary of the report can be found in *Facts on File, 1968*, pp. 78–86.

5. For a full account of events at the 1968 Democratic convention as compiled by the special subcommission of the National Commission on the Causes and Prevention of Violence, see Daniel Walker, *Rights in Conflict: the Violent Confrontation of Demonstrators and Police in the Parks and Streets of Chicago* (New York: Bantam Books, 1968). Again, an excellent summary of the report is available in *Facts on File, 1968*, pp. 357–382.

6. The court ruling in *Johnson* v. *Glick* is summarized in R. L. Worsnop, "Police Brutality," *CQ Researcher*,

September 6, 1991, p. 644 (published by *Congressional Quarterly*).

7. R. Sharpe, "Police Don't Discipline Themselves for Brutality," *Gannett News Service*, March 8, 1992.

8. J. DeParle, "To Criticism, U.S. Unveils Report on Police Brutality," *New York Times*, May 20, 1992, p. 18.

9. Quoted in J. McKinley, Jr. "Debate on New York Police Board Hits Up While Complaints Fall," *New York Times*, March 27, 1991.

10. Quoted in "Despite Reputation for Brutality, U.S. Police Seen Improving," *Reuters Newswire*, April 30, 1992.

11. R. L. Worsnop, p. 636.

12. W. A. Westley, "Violence and the Police," *American Journal of Sociology*, 1953, 59:34–41; reprinted in *Principles of Sociology* (2nd ed.), edited by K. Young and R. W. Mack (New York: American Book Company, 1962, pp. 264–272).

13. S. L. Brodsky and G. D. Williamson, "Attitudes of Police Toward Violence," *Psychological Reports*, 1985, 57, 1179–1180.

14. Quoted in D. K. Shah (interviewer), "Playboy Interview: Daryl Gates," *Playboy*, August 1991.

15. "Law and Disorder," *Time*, April 1, 1991, p. 18.

16. Quoted in R. L. Worsnop, p. 636.

17. Quoted in "Police Confront the Tough Issue of

Brutality: Has the Videotape of the King Beating Exposed a Dirty Little Secret? Or Is the Problem of Excessive Force Being Blown Out of Proportion? Experts' Opinions Differ Sharply," *Los Angeles Times,* April 4, 1991, p. A1.

18. Quoted in R. L. Worsnop, p. 638.

19. Ibid., p. 651.

Further Reading

Books

Kerner Commission. *Report on the National Advisory Commission on Civil Disorders.* New York: Bantam Books, 1968.

Smith, R. L. *The Tarnished Badge. New York: Crowell, 1965.*

Walker, D. *Rights in Conflict: The Violent Confrontation of Demonstrators and Police in the Parks and Streets of Chicago.* New York: Bantam Books, 1968.

Westley, W. A., *Violence and the Police.* Cambridge, Mass.: MIT Press, 1970.

Newspaper Articles

Chicago Tribune

Blau, R., and Jackson, D. "Brutality: A Festering Police Issue." Feb. 9, 1992, p. 1.

Grady, W. "Police Brutality Suit Heads to Trial." Feb. 15, 1989, p. 7.

Jackson, D. "Difficult Path to Justice in Cop Brutality Cases." May 3, 1992, p. 1.

Stein, S. "Burge Says No Torture Occurred." March 1, 1992.

Los Angeles Times

"The Rodney King Affair." March 3, 1991, p. B1.

Harrison, E. "Police Confront the Tough Issue of Brutality: Has the Videotape of the King Beating Exposed a Dirty Little Secret? Or Is the Problem of Excessive Force Being Blown Out of Proportion? Experts' Opinions Differ Sharply." April 4, 1991, p. A1.

Kopetman, R. "Charges Against Officers in Video 'Sting' Dismissed." May 14, 1991, p. A1.

Morley, J. "Patrick Murphy: One of Nation's Foremost Cops Brokenhearted by the Brutality." April 7, 1991, p. M3.

Serrano, R. A. "Police Documents Disclose Beating Was Downplayed." March 20, 1991, p. 1.

Serrano, R. A., and Wilkinson, T. "All 4 in King Beating Acquitted" April 30, 1992, p. 1.

Tobar, H., and Colvin, R. L. "Witnesses Depict Relentless Beating." March 7, 1991, Pt. B, p. 1.

Wallace, A., and Ferrell, D. "Verdicts Greeted With Outrage and Disbelief." April 30, 1992, p. 1.

New York Times

Bishop, K. "Police Attacks: Hard Crimes to Uncover, Let Alone Stop." March 24, 1991, p. 1.

Blumenthal, R. "Police Plan New Version of Foot Duty." Feb. 14, 1991.

Blumenthal, R. "Police Feel Haunted by Specter of Brutality." March 30, 1991, p. 21.

DeParle, J. "To Criticism, U.S. Unveils Report on Police Brutality." May 20, 1992, p. A18.

Hanley, R. "Officer Acquitted in Teaneck Killing." Feb. 12, 1992, p. A1.

Hanley, R. "Whereabouts of Gun Made Focus of Trial." Feb. 4, 1992, p. B1.

Lewis, N. A. "Police Brutality Under Wide Review By Justice Department." March 15, 1991.

McKinley, J. C., Jr. "Debate Over Police Review Board Heats Up While Complaints Fall." March 27, 1991, p. A1.

Mydans, S., et al. "Videotape of Beating by Officers Puts Full Glare on Brutality Issue." March 19, 1991, p. A1.

Prial, F. J. "Judge Acquits Sullivan in Shotgun Slaying of Bumpurs." Feb. 27, 1992, p. B1.

Reinhold, R. "Violence and Racism Are Routine In Los Angeles Police, Study Says." July 7, 1991, p. A1.

Reinhold, R. "City of Nightmares: A Terrible Chain of Events Reveals Los Angeles Without Its Makeup." May 3, 1992, Pt. 4, p. 1.

Roberts, S. "Brutal Question: Police Violence, Public Trust." March 25, 1991, p. 34.

Terry, D. "Kansas City Police Go After Own 'Bad Boys'." Sept. 10, 1991, p. A1.

Newsday

Moses, P. "Cop Brutality Settlements Cost City Millions in '90." April 30, 1991, p. 3.

USA Today

"Agreement on King." May 1, 1992, p. 4A.

Washington Post

Taylor, P., and Cannon, L. "King Chokes Back Tears, Calls for End to Violence; Beating Victim Asks End to Violence, Saying 'It's Just Not Right'." May 2, 1992, p. A1.

News Services

Sharpe, R. "Police Don't Discipline Themselves for Brutality." *Gannett News Service,* March 8, 1992.

Debusmann, B. "Despite Reputation for Brutality, U.S. Police Seen Improving." *Reuters,* April 30, 1992.

Periodicals

Brodsky, S. L., and Williamson, G. D. "Attitudes of Police Toward Violence." *Psychological Reports,* 1985, 57, 1179–1180.

Murphy, P. V. "How the Police View Violence." *New York State Journal of Medicine,* Feb. 1985.

Shah, D. K. (interviewer). "Playboy Interview: Daryl Gates." *Playboy,* August 1991.

Worsnop, R. L. "Police Brutality." *CQ Researcher,* September 6, 1991.

Newsweek

Baker, J. N., et al. "Los Angeles Aftershocks." April 1, 1991, p. 18.

Turque, B., et al. "Brutality on the Beat." March 25, 1991, p. 32.

Mathews, T., et al. "Fire & Fury: The Siege of L.A." May 11, 1992, p. 26.

Salholz, E., et al. "Blacks and Cops: Up Against a Wall." May 11, 1992.

Yocum, S. "Why It Happened: An L.A. Cop's View." March 25, 1991, p. 34.

Time

"More Hardball Ahead." April 8, 1991, p. 33.

Lacayo, R., et al. "Law and Disorder." April 1, 1991, p. 18.

Morrow, L. "Rough Justice." April 1, 1991.

Prud'Homme, A., et al. "Police brutality!" March 25, 1991, p. 16.

U.S. News & World Report

"A Rising Storm in L.A." March 25, 1991, p. 12.

Minerbrook, S. "A Different Reality for US." May 11, 1992, p. 36.

Gest, T., et al. "Why Brutality Persists." April 1, 1991, p. 24.

Witkin, G., et al. "What the LAPD Ought to Try." May 11, 1992, p. 27.

Index

111